OTHER BOOKS

BY

BOB THURBER

Nickel Fictions: 50 Exceedingly Brief Stories

Paperboy: A Dysfunctional Novel

Nickel Fictions: 50 Exceedingly Brief Stories
(VOLUME 1)

ISBN-13: 978-1466425125
ISBN-10: 1466425121

www.bobthurber.net

Thurber, Bob
Nickel Fictions, Volume 1

Nickel Fictions
50 Exceedingly Brief Stories

Bob Thurber

Recipient of
Over 50 Awards & Citations for Short Fiction

Author of
PAPERBOY: A Dysfunctional Novel

www.BobThurber.Net

"In the end, all books are written for your friends."
— Gabriel Garcia Marquez

Table of Contents

FOREWORD

Andrew Wilson

If you look for good short-short fictions either on the Web or in print, you'll spend plenty of time feeling annoyed. The flush of popularity enjoyed by the micro form is not yet translating into good stories. They're damned hard to write — that's one possible reason. The other is that most flash fiction writers have no idea of how to go about it. They tend to shrink big story concepts down, like t-shirts in a hot dryer. Voila, they say. A flash. It isn't.

Writers and critics of flash fiction pay lip service to tightness, compression, precision, and subtlety. As if we know by instinct what those are. One school says that the form is close to prose poetry and should not be forced to obey narrative logic. The other school insists on rudiments of plot. Adherents of both schools end up writing stories that, at 50-500 words, feel far too long, and are dispiriting and exhausting to read besides.

What's the problem? Maybe writers of these things are too busy with their intentions — and other associated conceptual straightjackets — to ride a wave (or a ripple) of language. You can feel the anxiety in their surrealistic contortions, misplaced ellipses, and truncated, mock-profound surprise endings. Also in the whiff of sensationalism that clings to so many flash fictions, and the oddly prim, proto-Hallmark morality.

No other literary form except haiku so rawly exposes a writer's weaknesses. You cannot hide behind a plot in short-short fiction, because the plot is only suggested. Your sentences are isolated in naked space, space that is terrifying since it cannot be improved upon. You can't distract readers with characters and runs of exposition. You don't even have time to develop an "original voice."

The only thing a flash fiction writer can do without boring us is to use that first sentence as a launching pad for leaping into space. Into orbit. *Veni, vidi, vici.* A fistful of words to light up the mind and the nervous system, each phrase stamped out to be as hard, impersonal and ringing as a coin.

In my literary career I've come across no more than a half dozen writers capable of writing literary micro fictions. Bob Thurber is the Maestro of these oddities, which in his characteristic style of self-deprecatory understatement he calls "nickel fictions." Pick up this book and see why."

-Andrew Wilson, October 4, 2011

PREFACE

Each of the selections in this collection has been previously published. And virtually all of them originally appeared in venues with strict word limits, some as high as 500 or 1000 words, some as low as 20 or 25. Tight spaces. Small canvases. Barely any room to breathe. Which is exactly how moments in real life can sometimes feel.

At one time or another some of these short-shorts have been called remarkable, masterful examples of micro-fiction. A few have been utilized in schools and universities as teaching tools and reference material, and at least one is still being used on reading assessment exams both in the US and abroad.

Those approving opinions, I understand, are entirely subjective. Anyone could argue (even protest) that the only thing remarkable about any of these exceedingly brief stories is that they take little time to read. Though some may take a bit longer to digest. Even so, some readers may ask: Okay, but where's the rest of it?

Frankly, there isn't any more. These small fictions are, for what they're worth, no more complex than little windup toys. They are miniatures, with minimal effects. And they are peepholes in an otherwise impenetrable wall. Consider them, if you will, simple mechanisms of the human heart with all its malfunctions.

Bob Thurber
www.bobthurber.net

INTRODUCTION

Vincent L. Carrella, Author of "Serpent Box"

Living is dangerous. Beyond tornadoes and car crashes, violence and disease. Living is fraught with cruelty and fear. It is not just what waits around the corner, it's often what lurks inside our own blackened hearts. The most terrible wars are sometimes fought within the walls of our own homes, and sometimes the people we love, the people who are supposed to love us, to protect us, cause the most damage, the most pain. Why is this so? We cannot understand the devil any more than we can hope to understand God. We are human. We are flawed. And we do things to ourselves and to each other that make no sense.

There are things that happen in this world that we'd rather not talk about. There are things that happen in safe, suburban neighborhoods that are still not commonly spoken. To ignore these things is to protect them. To avoid them is to avoid the truth. And the truth does hurt. The truth is uncomfortable and sometimes the truth is dangerous. And you don't have to face it. There are plenty of diversions for temporary relief and escape. This collection of stories is not one of them.

There are no feel-good endings here. Nothing is resolved. No moment is lived happily and there is no ever after. Nickel Fictions is a collection of startling, often uncomfortable slices of broken lives. People die here. People leave their children and sometimes hurt them. Faith lapses, violence looms and doom dangles like a dagger on a thread. These stories may be small, but each is pregnant with a bomb. Each is a moment of calm before a coming storm.

These are worlds, these stories. They're like port-holes in a ship of fools. Each one could be its own novel, it's own troubling little independent film. They fly by so quickly that you catch but mere glimpses of what's inside. But what you do see is marked by the slow-motion clarity of an unfolding tragedy. But through it all people do survive. They endure and persevere.

Living is dangerous, but it is also its own reward. And at the end of the day, we survive. Pain, and change is always coming but we were built to take it and Nickel Fictions is a testament to that strength.

———————————

Nickel Fictions

50 Exceedingly Brief Stories

———————————

Bob Thurber

LORD HAVE MERCY

His name is Roy Rogers — like the cowboy, like the restaurants — and he's old enough to be your father but you don't tell anyone you're dating a senior citizen you met on the bus because no one is going to meet Roy, not ever, especially your mother, so it's really none of their freaking business, though he, Roy, admits he's told everyone about you — friends, neighbours, anyone he meets, even strangers.

Roy is a nice enough guy, trim and fit, retired-movie-star-handsome, a widower who writes long letters and short poems to his dead wife, particularly when he gets tipsy; between weekly visits to her gravesite he likes to brag about robbing the cradle as though he seduced you and not the actuality, which is that you charmed and beguiled the poor fool, batting your lashes until the muscles in your eyes ached and he begged you for a dinner date.

What you are fairly certain Roy never tells anyone is that his pet name for you is Lolita L. Jailbait, a name you loathe and graciously ignored for a while because your mother taught you it is simply better to let annoying things fade and die lonely deaths. Besides being ridiculous, the name doesn't fit, because you're well past legal age and neither of you are breaking any laws, at least not state or federal.

When one Sunday you finally got around to asking him what the middle L stands for Roy said: Lord have mercy. He said it breathlessly, in a barely audible whisper, like a quiet prayer. And that put a slow burn in your belly, producing an uncomfortable heat that made you blush and smile so wide you couldn't help showing your teeth which are slightly crooked though only by millimetres and should, one orthodontist told you, eventually correct themselves, though to your eye, in your most candid opinion, they are gradually getting worse, particularly the front two which appear to be wrestling with one another in slow-motion.

When Roy isn't in the room you sometimes catch yourself practicing in front of the mirror, shifting your jaw, trying to align your bite, presenting fake smiles beneath weary eyes that contain a flat, dull, heartless look. And that's the real problem, isn't it: your heart is shrinking, getting smaller every day, and you blame your father, that prick, and in a covert way you blame Roy, especially when you catch him crying on days he calls Anniversaries: departed wife's birthday, wedding day, date of death, other times that Roy won't elaborate upon.

Once he openly wept while you had his dick in your mouth and you had to muster all your strength not to bite down and create a permanent wound. Poor Roy. He's such a wimpy lover. He seldom initiates. His hands tremble noticeably when you finger the buttons on his shirt, not unbuttoning, merely fiddling while you rest your head on his chest, gauging his heartbeat as you gaze, slightly upward, careful to avoid the center of his pinched, downward stare.

Afterwards, when he races for the bathroom, you sometimes look at Roy's naked back and try to imagine your father leaving your room at night. The same narrow-shoulders, same nubby spine like some reptilian fossil is nestled there, though your father was taller by a foot and never had a single grey hair. It's at moments like these that you understand why your heart is shrivelling up, shrinking at an alarming rate, and just like your broken smile there isn't a thing you can do to save it.

MASQUERADE

Halloween night, a month before he shoots himself in the face, my brother Charles dresses as Death. I suit up as a chicken. My cheap plastic beak looks so lame that I tape a Playtex rubber glove to my chin. Charles shades his eyes with grease paint. He smudges his face with charcoal gray until his features disappear.

How do I look, he says, grinning in the shadow of his hooded cloak. He moves a fluorescent bone, formerly an arm, and practices a maniacal laugh. His hand is one long crooked finger. He moves straight toward me, reaching, stretching the laugh out. He wiggles the cold tip of eternity in my face and the cheap rubber band on my beak snaps. Charles helps me fix it with Scotch tape and string but the beak doesn't sit right.

The party is six houses down so we don't drive. We cut across two lawns and climb a fence, Death and I. Everyone guesses my identity right away, even dumb Johnny who is dressed as Goldilocks and the 3 bears. Nobody bats an eye at Charles.

I'm sorry, what are you supposed to be, a girl with yarn hair and painted freckles says to me.

Charles wins Most Original and Best Costume, which turns out to be one prize. A queen with lacquered braids and a glittered crown kisses him on the mouth. The rest of the night Goldilocks and the 3 Bears snub him. Dorothy, cradling a stuffed Toto, curses behind Death's back. When we leave a man wrapped in foil tips his tea kettle hat and hands each of us a bag of candy corn.

Charles eats half his bag on the walk home.

Weeks later, days before they find him, I wake in the pitch black wondering if I spoke out loud until my mother, huddled in the doorway, her hand on the light switch, says: What, what is it, what did you dream?

MY NEW PLACE

My new place was a furnished room (bed, dresser, chair) with a slanted ceiling, above a brick-front thrift shop called Bargain Plus. The weekend I moved in, the shop was running a two-for-one sale on solid oak picture frames, all shapes and sizes.

After I unloaded my car, I went downstairs and blew money that I couldn't afford to blow. But I know quality when I hold it in my hand.

All that night, instead of unpacking, I sat on the floor sorting, snipping, and framing. By midnight I had my kids up on the wall. All my kids, in all shapes and sizes. And I had them at all the ages I had known, ages they would never be again. I had them with pets and people who had died. I made an arrangement. It was easy. A dozen nails, about a dozen, most of them painted over, were already in the wall. I hammered in a half dozen more.

I arranged my life on that wall.

"Hey asshole," my new neighbour said. He banged five, six times from his side. "How do you like it?"

Of course I didn't. The wall shook, the man sounded drunk, and I didn't like the way he made the children's pictures jump.

By closing my eyes I am back in that place, on that bed, clutching my pillow like it is a human form.

FLOAT

When we heard the horn, we all started down together. My mother led the way. She only had the one suitcase, but she made a big show of dragging it down the two flights one stair at a time in front of my father and me, and an even bigger show about fitting it in the car.

The man she was running away with sat behind the wheel and made no effort to help. He had his door open, both feet in the road. His eyes were very round, very large. I stood stiff and quiet beside my father and the man looked over at us. His hair was rough cut and longer than mine and he didn't seem old enough to be my mother's lover. He didn't appear more than five or six years older than me. She kept talking at him while she struggled with her suitcase but the man stayed focused. He worked a cigarette and kept his eyes mostly on my father.

After she settled onto the front seat and secured her door, she said something to the man who closed his door and said something back to her. He tossed his cigarette out his side window then gave the car a little gas, moving them slowly, slower than a float in a parade, so there was plenty of time for anything to happen, certainly enough time for my mother to turn and wave.

Near the end of our street the driver raced to make the light. The tires squealed and the rear of the car bounced as my mother and her lover rocketed through the intersection.

"Well that's that," my father said. His hand came down heavy on my shoulder. "Good riddance," he said, and I felt the tremor in his fingers as he kneaded the flesh between my bones. "I don't wish her any bad luck." He held me firm, kept me from turning. "Well, what was I supposed to say?"

SOMETHING TO REMEMBER YOU BY

My father's taxi arrived early, a full hour ahead of schedule. The driver blasted the horn continuously until Dad, carrying a single suitcase, ran out to talk with him. All the rest of his luggage — everything except his camera equipment — was packed in a leather trunk and a few boxes stacked beside the garage. He spoke with the driver then came back inside.

"Okay, my ride's here, so let's do this." He sounded out of breath. "Act natural, now. I want a decent shot." He made an adjustment to the tripod then peeked above the camera. "Eyes front. No posing."

Mom sighed from the sofa. "Trust me, dear, no one feels like posing." She straightened her back, crossed her legs.

My father aligned his face with the viewfinder. "That's posing! Fix your skirt."

Mom's eyes shifted over to me.

"You're scaring the boy," she said.

"The hell I am." He snapped his fingers. "Look at me, not at him."

I shifted my feet as Mom hunched forward, spilling cleavage, smiling, showing all her teeth.

"Kill the happy face," my father said. "I'm wise to your tricks."

I moved toward his side of the camera until I could see what he was seeing.

"Snap it, then," my mother said. "Take your god damn picture and go." Her cheeks were flushed red. Lines appeared on her forehead.

Another step and I had the same angle as him. I made a frame of my hands, thumbs touching. Mom cranked up the intensity of her stare, Her cheeks hollow, her mouth a flat line. "That's it, that's perfect. There's the woman I'm leaving," my father said.

DUCK WALK

The moment I got off the phone with the mortgage people, my mood turned black. I thought I was going to faint. Then I heard the girls shriek and the screen door slam. I pasted on a crooked smile, laced up my dancing shoes, hurried downstairs.

Ann was frying eggs in a skillet. The eggs were for her and me.

Third night in a row we'd fed the girls early, giving them French toast and orange juice, then let them run wild outside, inside, upstairs and down.

Ann jerked the pan, flipped the eggs like a sauté chef. "What did they say?"

I put the cap on a bottle of fake syrup.

"Recording gives their office hours, that's all. I'll call tomorrow from work."

"Look at me," Ann said.

I pushed some plates around. Then I climbed over a chair and pinched a half of soggy toast off the tray of Janet's highchair. "How come Janet didn't finish?"

"Look this way, please."

I looked, but briefly. My eyes wouldn't hold steady.

"Oh, my. I know that look," Ann said. "How bad is it?"

"This look," I said showing her my teeth.

"For your information, Mister Gloom. I'm more worried about you than I am about them taking the house."

I licked my fingers. They were horribly sweet.

"No one is taking the house," I said.

She brought the eggs to me. "Tell it straight. None of your sideshow acts. I want to know."

I distorted my face — long chin, stiff tongue, goofball eyes. I rolled my eyes, made my ears wiggle. I pushed my stomach into a bulge. Then I squatted, hands on my hips, elbows sharp.

Ann said: "Please stop."

The kids stampeded in. Two of them shrieked. All of them laughed at Daddy, funny Daddy.

Ann tried to shoo the girls away, but I wiggled a duck walk. I flapped my arms and they screamed. They made a circle. I wagged and quacked. They clapped and giggled. I fell over, trembling, sobbing at their mother's feet.

They couldn't stop laughing.

DEATHBED NOTES OF AN OLD QUEER PRIEST

How disappointing to discover so late in life that the angel of death's flirtations remain indifferent to my sins. God in all his glory has no love for the unclean, unbaptised. This unpalatable news arrives late one evening while I'm sipping sacrament wine from a Dixie cup, years after all my boys deserted me — all those fine young men I found by sound (and lured with subtle rhyming schemes) mere children, most of them abandoned or homeless runaways, to whom I spoon fed beef broth and oyster crackers, while sharing my steamy jokes, all the while pumping cheap port wine straight into their veins, chuckling to myself to let the little darlings know it was desirable to laugh — preferable, in fact — and to stop being for Christ's sake so God awful nervous.

A seductive toss of wet hair worked, back when I had enough hair to toss, because they weren't stupid, these street urchins, these roughnecks, but who on Earth keeps a scorecard, and what did it matter so long as they ended up bathed, scrubbed spotless for the night, surface clean, their shapely legs shaved bare.

With some I'd drag a razor across their chests, up and over and beneath their thin arms, along frail shoulders, (the hard cases, honey-waxed in the coarsest spots) then set to work on their filthy, tangled hair, which I methodically shampooed and lathered into streaming silk. Blown dry and combed, their heavy eyelashes shadowing curious glances, their angular faces frozen as I persuaded them to slip into pleated pink dresses over girdles with garters and black seamed stockings. Garments that had outlived mother, God rest the soul of that venomous whore. Once adorned, each lad cooperated, making me his primary and immediate business, the shy ones generally more eager than the rest.

Dulled by drink and a slip of a pill, they allowed me to trace two halves of a cupid arrow across their heart-shaped asses after I painted their faces, made them pretty with accents and highlights, demonstrating the art of crisp outline with soft blends and pastel shades.

Those with long fingers and slender hands I manicured, building length with a quick hardening gel, then painted their shapely nails blood red. The rest was all their doing, all their idea, the clawing at my bottomless itch. I never hinted, never unzipped, never initiated, never settled with any sum, cash check or charge.

One boy (you'll laugh) some Butch or Buster or Buck, found me in the city, who knows how, climbed three stories of rain gutter to my loft, in August heat no less. (Lean close: You'll get such a chuckle.) Crashing into my studio in mud-stained work-boots and denim overalls with a rawhide belt of shiny tools, he slashed a couch pillow to get my full attention. Feathers floated in the air. I gasped, feigning fear, thinking here is something new, something fresh, and gasped again, figuring a formal execution was now taking place. Or a burglary, by God, who knew.

I didn't recall his face or beauty, or the tiny curved scar on his forehead like a crescent moon, not a hint without the yellow tresses and makeup. His skull hairless except for a gray shadow, the same sandpaper length as his beard.

Kiss me, he said. Kiss my mouth.

Here? I said, Now?

Don't you remember this mouth, Father. You called it sweet once.

But try as I might, I could not recall.

Then he said: I came to murder you tonight, not just once, but as many times as you murdered me. Do you remember murdering me, Father?

He is being metaphorical, I thought, as well as coy; but after a dozen tiny deaths spilled upon the alter of his quick and calloused hands I did at last remember, as clearly as I would a lost and forgotten son, and in that fleeting moment life, my life, at long last seemed fair.

GRAYS

First payday after he got fired Ray filtered in with the third shift crowd like he was still one of them. I saw him squeeze into a spot at the end of the bar, but I didn't say anything. Ray was Ray and he wasn't going to change. He had a bent and crooked nose from crashing a forklift into a vending machine but he could smell fresh money and free drinks.

But then he started passing around his photos, the black and white spy shots of his daughter taking a shower. He had a dozen glossy pictures of her wet and dry, semi-nude, slick and shiny, shots of her with a towel wrapped like a turban; other shots with her hair hanging loose and wet. She was eighteen or nineteen, red haired and freckled, already married, with a child of her own.

"How much," he said, "for the complete set?

The factory crowd wasn't buying. A few guys flipped though the whole stack but showed no real interest.

"See me on pay day," said one fat son of a bitch.

Ray collected and counted the photos. He looked beat. His hands were shaking. I waited on everybody else, then I stood in front of Ray. He raised his head up as I poured him a double shot of the good stuff.

"What's this for? You don't like me," he said.

He fingered a scar on the back of his hand that his ex-wife had supposedly put there with a claw hammer. Ray was not a photographer any more than I was a bartender, and though I didn't agree with the subject matter of his pictures, he had managed to capture a nice mix of light and shadow.

"I still don't like you," I said. "But you held your greys."

GRAVE INVITATION

Death wore an overcoat to my mother's funeral. He wore a Russian-style hat with fur flaps turned down, a red scarf, and fuzzy green mittens. A heavy snow slanted down on the wind. Behind us on the hill the entire procession sat waiting in steaming cars.

"How long you staying," I asked Death.

The wind changed direction, whipping snow against my face.

I said, "We have food and drink in a nice rented hall. It's not much. Chicken and ham salad. Assorted cheeses with crackers, pickles, olives. Some sliced fruit. You're welcome to join us," I said.

I waited for Death to make up his mind.

After a good long while my wife trudged down the hill, her scarf streaming like a banner.

"Don't do this to yourself," she said.

LAST TIME I SAW MY FATHER

A match flame lit up his face in the window, a cigarette clenched in the center of his mouth, his eyes brilliant with fire. The flame vanished and only the orange dot of his cigarette remained, dancing close to the glass like a bumbling firefly.

THE LION TAMER'S WIFE

On a moonless August night when I was twelve, I climbed a wall of hay bundles stacked beside the elephant's pen and from that high perch witnessed six clowns, one of them a midget, one of them a mute, all taking turns screwing the lion tamer's wife, Nadya, that skinny, trapeze whore, Russian gymnast, Olympic failure, who would do anything for a pint of cheap vodka. I watched two clowns mount her, one after the other, then pull up their suspender-pants, at which point the midget clown handed each a fat cigar.

I ran to find my father, as I had always been instructed to report anything unusual that I observed. I found him by the chimpanzee cages, sitting on a milk crate. He was shirtless, still wearing his red britches and black knee-high boots.

When I was close enough to shout I saw he was puffing the stub of a fat cigar, blowing perfect smoke rings at a baby chimp that my mother, the fat lady, had named Caesar. At that moment I heard my mother calling my name, so I swallowed my secret, felt it burn my throat and drop into my belly like a stone, as I ran frantically toward our trailer, our little home on wheels, every part of me aching to be smothered by the soft, warm folds of my sweet mother's flabby arms.

I never spoke another word to my father. Not one. Not even after I had my turn with the lion tamer's wife who referred to me only as The Quiet Boy. I seldom spoke to anyone but my mother, and after she died of a heart attack I conversed only with Caesar, that clever chimp, whom I trained to light my cigars.

BIOLOGY LESSON

I watched him dig the heart out. The trap's metal bar had snapped the mouse's neck. The heart was the size of a raisin. My father pinched it with the tweezers and held it close to my face.

"See that," he said "They're all like that."

Then he put it with the rest, in his jar of little hearts.

MINIMALISM AT THE BEACH

Carol turned her sun burnt back to the ocean. She huddled against the wind and lit a cigarette with the burning filter of Anna's cigarette.

Breeze bumped past and hooked her sunglasses on Ginger's bikini top.

"Don't lose those. They're my dads'. I'm going in."

"You're going swimming?" Anna said.

"What's wrong with swimming," Ginger said.

Carol streamed smoke at the three girls.

Breeze said, "I'm going to paddle out and try to not get my hair wet. How's it look?"

"It's too short," Ginger said.

"Watch for the undertow." Anna said.

"Stop saying it's short, you guys! Tell me really."

"I hate it," Carol said. "I'm being totally honest. It makes you look wicked fat."

Breeze said, "Liar, liar. All liars go to hell. Okay. Bye Bye."

"It's gorgeous darling," Ginger called through funneled hands.

The three girls watched Breeze run, hop, spin, wave.

"She only can't swim a stroke," Anna said.

"What do you think?" Ginger said.

"That hair suffered a severe chemical burn," said Anna. "This sun isn't going to help."

"Who could blame her if she filled her belly with stones," Carol said.

Anna said, "On the way to get you guys she told me he's still bothering her like almost every night and doing you know what every chance he gets. She says she wants to seriously hurt herself."

"Good," said Carol. "We'll all watch."

CRYBABIES

It was never explained why our mother left us, or when she might return. Every other week father showed us a new letter and then read it aloud, which didn't take more than a minute because they were always short, a single typed page, with no signature.

He told us he destroyed the envelopes so that we couldn't see the return address.

"Can't have the three of you chasing after your mommy like a bunch of crybabies," he said.

From these letters we heard about the exotic places our mother visited and her many adventures.

Each letter ended the same: All my love to all my darlings.

After every reading a small war broke out.

"When is she coming home," my sister said.

"Does she miss any of us," my brother said. "She never says she misses me."

"Why doesn't she ever send a picture," I asked.

Father answered each inquiry with the same stern reply: "Write and ask. I'll mail your letters. I'll send her anything you want to say."

In this way we learned to compose long heartfelt letters full of wonder and concern.

DOCTOR ARCADE

The very first time my mother frightened me, I woke in mid air. I was just that small a bundle. She swept me up from my crib, tossed me toward the ceiling, wiggled and shook until I laughed, until I wailed and screamed. Until I pissed all over myself.

I told that story to a doctor and he said he could cut that memory right out of me, zap it with a laser, honest to God, remove that horror and other horrors of equal magnitude. In strict layman terms: a sophisticated computer told the laser precisely where to go.

Other motherly memories wouldn't be damaged, though some might become hazy, he said, a slight motherly fog, but overall he'd need my help, my undivided attention for the next year of my life and of course full payment in advance, personal check just fine, total cost twelve to sixteen thousand, make the check out for twelve and we'll bill for the rest, ha ha! That's one year, two sessions a week. No refunds. Think about it. One year. You walk away a new man.

I never believed in helping myself beyond what my pocketbook could afford, but the Doc looked like such a fun loving sharp shooting professional, I couldn't wait to get him on the computer end of a laser with my brain cells dancing in the cross hairs.

WISHES

For a long time he sat and watched her and she said nothing, and that was all right by him. The less trouble the better.

He watched her smoke. He watched her pace to the window and back. He watched her cross and uncross her legs and smooth her nylons and examine her nails and puff small white smoke rings toward the high ceiling.

After a time she said, "What do you say we talk about something else."

She was smirking. "So what do you do when you're not guarding crazy women?"

He grinned. He couldn't help grinning.

She said: "I bet you get some kind of bonus for keeping your mouth shut?"

"Is that the case," she said.

"Does my husband offer you those kind of incentives," she said.

When he didn't answer, she opened a magazine and turned the page. She turned the pages too fast to be reading. Each time she turned a page she dangled her shoe on the end of her foot.

He wished he had a magazine for himself, a magazine and a cigarette. He wished he had a drink. He wished it was the end of his shift instead of the middle. He wished he owned a chair as comfortable as the one he was sunk into. He wished his wife looked like this woman, just a little, some small resemblance, so he could go home and make love to her and watch the changes in her face.

He wished and wished.

SHUTEYE

The yellow light over the stove gave the air an amber glow. Donna had my heart on the table and a steak knife in her hand. I bumped something in the shadows by the door and she quickly put down the knife and covered everything with a dish towel. But I know my heart when I see it, I know my heart even in dim light.

"You're up," she said.

"So are you. What day is it?"

She pulled her wristwatch from the pocket of her robe.

"Four hours into Thursday. I got up with the baby."

"Oh," I said. "I didn't hear."

I stepped to one side of the table and Donna moved with me.

"I know," she said. "She was wet, soaked all the way through. So I changed her, and fed her, then rocked her. She took half a bottle. Dead to the world now, thank god. You should climb back into dreamland."

"Why?"

"Too early to be up."

"You're up."

"Only because I woke up," she said, "and not by choice."

I stepped to the other side of the table and Donna moved with me. She dropped her watch into her pocket.

"Go on. Grab some shuteye. You look awful."

"Do I?"

She nodded with great enthusiasm. I wondered if she'd already had coffee. I thought about making some, starting my day.

"What have you got there?"

Her eyebrows danced. "Where?"

"On the table."

"I'm making your lunch," she said.

"My lunch?"

"Just because you work in a restaurant doesn't mean you have to eat the food there. Now go," she said. "I'll be in soon as I've cleaned up here."

I didn't move. Neither did she. In the next room the baby made a noise, a little cough like a faraway owl. I looked at the table, at the lump my heart made in the dishtowel.

"I'm going to make coffee," I said. "You want some?"

"Oh you don't want to do that. Trust me," Donna said. "You'll be a much happier man without coffee and with a couple more hours of shuteye."

But I didn't see how that was possible, how I could do any of those things—close my eyes, go to sleep, trust my wife, or ever be happy again.

NEW MOTHER

She walked for hours through drifting snow. The overhead branches looked black against the pale sky. She wanted to find the exact spot where she and the young soldier had made love, beneath a wide tree where he had carved their initials inside a heart-shape.

But the pain soon became too much for her to bare.

She braced against a tree, felt her water break. She squatted and pushed.

The agony was too much and she cried out. Several hard pushes later, the child came right out.

She had felt all along it would be a boy, but she examined it to make sure. Then she cut him loose, wrapped him in her coat and laid him at the foot of the tree.

It was a good warm coat that the soldier had given her and she was sorry to lose it.

THREE DAYS OF MOURNING

On the third day the old man took down a haunch of cooked beef hanging from the cabin's ceiling. The blade of his knife was razor-thin and passed through the meat without resistance. He was sixty years old and in mourning for his wife whose body still lay on the bed. He had been drinking for three days without sleep and now he needed to eat.

He set himself a place at the table. He ate slowly, chewing each bite twenty times. The meat tasted dry and salty.

As he ate he stared straight ahead at the stone fireplace which took up one wall. When he finished eating he would fetch a shovel and go to work.

His wife had died peacefully in her sleep, and he imagined that was not a hard way to go. When his time came he believed very little effort would be necessary.

Anatomy of "Three Days of Mourning."

The text contains eleven sentences, each performing a small structural task. Though each sentence doesn't don't do much, in combination they produce a small emotional effect.

1) On the third day the old man took down a haunch of cooked beef hanging from the cabin's ceiling.

Introduction of Time, Character, Place, and Main Prop — the "haunch of cooked beef."

2) The blade of his knife was razor-thin and passed through the meat without resistance.

Character in action with Main Prop.

3) He was sixty years old and in mourning for his wife whose body still lay on the bed.

Physical and mental characteristics, and present situation.

4) He had been drinking now for three days without sleep and now he wanted to eat.

Character's reaction to event, and proposed goal.

5) He set himself a place at the table.

Character in action, moving toward goal

6) He ate slowly, chewing each bite twenty times.

Character in action with Main Prop.

7) The meat tasted dry and salty.

Character's sensory reaction to Main Prop.

8) As he ate he stared straight ahead at the stone fireplace which took up one wall.

Character's reflective delay.

9) When he finished he would fetch a shovel and go to work.

Character's proposed new goal.

10) His wife had died peacefully in her sleep, and he imagined that was not a hard way to go.

Character's reflection.

11) When his time came he believed very little effort would be necessary.

Character's emotional response, in summary, understated.

MEMBRANE

Even though the oxygen tank had been turned off, the Hospice nurse said there was no smoking allowed inside my mother's apartment, so I stepped out into the hallway and paced with the unlit cigarette dangling from my mouth.

Other people came and went. I stayed in the hall, letting them have their time.

It was my last cigarette, and I didn't light it. I wanted to save it for later when I would really need a smoke. I simply paced the hall with the cigarette hanging from my mouth.

When the nurse stuck her head out to alert me that the time was near and I should come in, I ripped the cigarette from my mouth. I felt the skin on my bottom lip tear away. Not a lot of skin, just a thin layer of tissue, but enough to make my mouth sting as I leaned over to kiss my mother goodbye.

When I was twelve, I kissed a schoolgirl in the balcony of the public library, an awkward, unsatisfying kiss that was a prelude to our breaking up.

This felt just like that. Almost.

A YARD FULL OF BIRDS

Sunday, after church, I woke in Harold's big chair, surrounded by long shadows. I had a sense of dreaming something the minister had said. A sea breeze puffed the curtains at me. I moved my head a tiny bit, just enough to see what had become of the sun. And what I saw pulled my breath from me: our entire yard overrun with birds. Hundreds of small black birds hopping about, pecking the ground between the patch that had once been my garden all the way back to the pines.

"Harold, come quick. Bring my glasses!"

I got to my feet and stood behind the curtain. It took nearly a minute before it settled on me.

So often after a nap I remember like that: too late, so sudden. No more Harold. No Harold to bring anything to or from. The idea settles and resettles like a familiar ache. Too often now I lose my senses and find myself talking to empty space. That's not entirely my fault. The house is too large for one person. Last Sunday I thought about baking a French meat pie and planning a picnic lunch for two. I spoke to the house. I addressed the house as Harold. I heard the echo.

A little of that is fine, my daughter-in-law tells me; completely normal for a woman my age; though too much, she doesn't say this on the phone, too much might start me down trouble's road, make more of a problem than I am worth.

The truth is I'd hate to be a bother, to her or my son. Toward the end of his days Harold despised that he had become a bother to doctors and nurses, children and friends. You are no bother, Harold, I used to tell him. He was no bother. Not for one moment to the very end. Though I agree a burden to one's children is no proud way to finish a life.

By feel alone I found my reading glasses among my knitting, and then my good distance glasses in the very next place I looked. The curtain puffed up and pressed across my face. I held it like a veil and I focused on the birds. I considered all the birds. I doubted anyone, especially my daughter-in-law would believe so many birds alighted in one small space. So I took a count. I used my finger. I tallied up and across. I calculated, and reached an estimate just seconds before they broke, all of them, rising, their flickering shadows curling over the house like a giant black wave.

The fluttering boomed like thunder.

Oh, Harold! My precious darling. These eyes are bad and my numbers may be off — way off. Please take a count from your side. Do tell me you saw what I saw, just now: between the pines and the patch that was the garden, more than enough birds to mask the face of God.

BALLOON MAN

Next morning the balloon man is still there: old guy in suspender overalls, standing beside his balloon cart on the corner opposite from where I catch the bus to the First Baptist Church. He looks completely out of place now that the street sweepers have come and gone, now that the yellow sawhorses and detour signs have all been removed. The street lights hold a glow beneath this drab summer sky. And everything has a predawn downtown-Sunday-sameness, except the balloon man is on the corner, still working, hissing helium from a torpedo-sized tank, making each new balloon squeal before tying it off with a length of precut string. My bus comes, and I board. I don't recognize the driver, so I don't sit up front. As I'm pulled forward, out my window I see the flat look of indifference on the old man's face as he casually allows another balloon to rise above his head and bump with the rest.

THE LAST TRASH CAN

We went to climb a mountain, a small mountain. A two-mile hike. She had hiked a mountain or two prior, and I had done a few half-mountains with the Scouts, but this was our first mountain together. We planned to kiss at the summit. She didn't know about the ring.

To be safe we had each invited a pair of friends to climb along and witness our affections, and to help carry sandwiches, water and wine, and add to the general spirit and to the joy.

Plus, I wanted pictures taken of me proposing on one knee.

In a clearing marked "Last Trash Can" we broke for lunch. Cold air swallowed us up. People and warnings started floating down. Hikers wound past us, shouting downhill. The weather had shifted. There was ice and snow above the tree line. Ruddy-faced climbers with backpacks and knitted caps turned back. We had nothing. We were six kids in denim jackets. We were children.

BLIND DATE

In the last days of my father's life, when it no longer made any difference to anyone, we invited both my parents to Sunday dinner. I rented a van to pick dad up. I had to sign for him like he was a package.

Mother, the last to arrive, twisted out of her coat.

Her lipstick was crooked. A purple veil hung from her purple hat.

She hissed her speech, as though suddenly my half-deaf father could hear from rooms away.

If once in his life he said what he came to say, I'd listen, she said. You know I would, if for no better reason then to hear him out. I would sit down, shut up and listen. But you know how he is when he gets up on his high horse. Is that his car at the curb — the fancy red one?

I said: Mom. He's eighty-seven years old.

She said: That time I went to visit he drove over my foot in his wheel chair. On purpose.

I said: Mom, be nice.

She said: I'm here, I'm civil, that should be enough.

I said: Mom. Please.

She said: Forty-four years every night he woke me with his nasal drip. That should be enough.

I said: Mom, please. He's waiting.

She looked at me like I was wavering out of focus.

He's a good-for-nothing, always was. He should be out here, greeting me himself, kissing my hand if not my feet.

He's by the fire, I said. The children like looking at him. Carol is showing photos of when I used to take baths in scuba gear.

I took those photos, my mother said. Every one. He never once watched you dive in the tub. He'd never allow it.

Then she leaned on my arm: You don't know. This better be enough for him. All the nice he expects of me, being what we are together. What we grew to become. Love is hard. You can't possibly understand. Ask him. Ask your father. Don't listen to a word I've said.

SIGNAL FIRE

Edgar, the night watchman leans over the edge of the roof and flings his cigarette down into the alley between the bank and my father's restaurant, just missing the fry grease barrel, exploding sparks against the screen door to the kitchen, where I'd be standing, looking up, if I hadn't climbed the fire escape to bring him coffee.

"You're a special kind of woman, Rose," he says, and I blush, fingering my name tag, shaking my hair loose, hiding my age and my innocence in the shadows of the moon.

DAY 59

I woke with chest pain, dull but deep. I was soaked with sweat. The blankets had been peeled back and I was shivering with cold. In the kitchen my new wife had my heart out on the table. She was wearing a lobster bib and welder's goggles. She jabbed a fork in, sawed with a steak knife.

"Whoa," I said. "Easy there."

That was one day, one incident.

The whole marriage was like that.

HER EX-BOYFRIEND'S EMAIL

At first I thought nothing of it.

Then, a few days later, I asked her if I could read it.

She said, "Read what?"

I said, "His email."

She said, "What email? Who are you talking about?"

I said, "You know who."

And I winked though I am not and have never been a winker.

She said, "Oh. That." And she made a sour face. "He didn't say much."

And I might have let it go at that, if she hadn't turned her face away, eyes narrowed, jaw stiff, lips tight.

"C'mon," I said, "Bring it up on the screen."

She said, "I think I deleted it".

I said, "No you didn't. Why would you delete it?"

She shrugged. "I don't know. I read it then I deleted it."

I said, "But you never delete your emails".

She shrugged again.

I said, "You've got emails that go back years, emails you've saved forever."

She said nothing.

I said, "Why delete this one?"

She said, "I don't know. I didn't think about it. After I read the thing I just clicked the delete button and it was gone."

I tilted my head and looked at her hard. I stared and said nothing for a long while.

She said, "The button is right there, you know, big as life".

That's when I said, "I know exactly where the damn button is."

HEART

I was dreaming of my dead mother when my wife woke me complaining of soreness in her chest. She put the light on, bunched her nightgown up to her neck, trapped it there with her chin.

Here, she said. Feel.

She guided my hand beneath her breast. I watched her eyes.

We had been married forever — more years than I was able to calculate, or categorize, or comprehend. We had seen our children grow and marry and have children of their own.

Feel anything, she said.

My fingers pulsed with the rhythm of her heart.

In that moment I felt my entire life fluttering just out of reach, fading like a shadow caught in sudden fierce light

I said, No, nothing. You're fine. Go back to sleep.

But when I took my hand away, I felt my own heart thrashing about, gasping like a fish flung from cool ocean surf onto bone white blistering sand.

DIRTY LAUNDRY

One Saturday, shortly after all the papers had been filed and we were just waiting for the court to make it official, she called and said, What are you doing?

I said, Laundry. Why?

She said, Feel like chatting?

And I suspected then she had been drinking.

Where's the baby, I said.

At my mother's, why?

How is she, I said.

We're all absolutely fine, thank you for asking.

And that came out bitter, like she wasn't quite drunk enough.

So I explained how things worked with a shared laundry room in a house with eight other tenants.

Oh, poor you, she said.

I said, Is there something special you wanted?

And she said, Yeah. I wanted you to know that somehow someway I'm going to make you fall in love with me again.

What would be the point of that, I said.

Just to make you hurt, she said.

ABSOLUTION

We were chatting about the divorce, how things would be after. I forget what I said. It was nothing out of the ordinary. But she slapped me. Right there in front of the kid.

I could take a slap in those days. It didn't faze me. I didn't do more than blink.

After a long silence she raised her arm like she was winding up for a second shot, then slowly brought her hand to her mouth. Tears streamed down her cheeks.

"Hurt your hand?" I said.

She nodded, trembling all over.

"Let me see."

"It's all right," she said.

"Let me have a look."

She shook her head no, then extended the hand, limp, listless.

I held it, rubbed my thumb across her knuckles, then turned it over and looked at her palm.

"It's red, but it seems all right. Try moving your fingers."

She moved one after another, until she'd moved them all, then nodded. Her eyes looked raw and wet.

"I'll never forgive you," she said.

"I know."

HISTORY LESSON

Our first weekend back from the honeymoon we went to a Chinese restaurant on Mineral Spring Avenue in Pawtucket. We sat in a padded booth, staring at each other across the Formica tabletop with our place mats showing the signs of the Chinese zodiac. I remember her lighting a cigarette in that hollow-cheek fashion she always used to light her cigarettes, every one. Streaming smoke at me, she said, "Why the look?" and I kept staring, trying to balance the corners of my face, thinking, God damn, this crude smile is going to collapse and give me away, tip my hand, reveal my true feelings. And that was the first time I admitted to myself that we weren't going to make it, no matter what I said. So I recorded that moment like a history lesson, taking special note of the brief life we had shared.

NEVER IN A MILLION YEARS

I was admiring the garnish on the soup du jour when my husband's whore came in with her mother.

— That's her, Scott said.

We were at a small round table with a view of the putting green. Scott had the tasseled leather wine list open but he wasn't exactly hiding behind it. Between us was a giant sandwich in the shape of a football. The toothpicks were tiny team banners.

— Never in a million years would I have guessed she'd show up here, Scott said.

I strained my neck.

— Which one is she? Not the silver fox, I said, playing dumb.

Because I never dreamed she'd be so young.

— Don't do anything foolish, Scott said. Be cool, now. We don't want to cause a scene.

The hostess led them directly toward our table. The mother was clearly a superior woman, neatly dressed, middle-aged regal, with a dainty nose and a stately manner. All the girl really had going for her was a mop of bleach blonde hair and a chest she'd one day regret. It was small comfort to discover she was not the sickly waif I'd been informed about, that her face contained too many clashing pastels to be appealing. I watched her charcoal-ringed eyes as she passed. Her hoop earrings were as big as handcuffs.

Scott was pinching the side of his mustache. He appeared antsy. For a few heartbeats she had been close enough to touch.

— Well, that was certainly an anxious few seconds, Scott said.

I could have pushed a fork through his throat.

REPEAT AS NECESSARY

I woke up hard, my pretty wife punching me. We were outside, in an alley, brick all around.

— You bastard, you no good son of a bitch!

She had her knee in my chest. She was shrieking, swinging wildly, landing clean shots to my face and head. Blood began leaking out of my nose. I got to my knees and grabbed hold of one arm, then the other. She kicked as I tried to hold on. I hadn't eaten in days, and all my instincts, all my reflexes were off.

— What's this about, I said.

She head-butted me. Dead solid perfect. I heard something in my face crack.

— Hey, whoa, stop a minute, I said. What the hell did I do?

She brought her knee up and slammed her shin into my groin.

— Bastard!

I went down. I fell hard.

I woke with two harsh white suns in my eyes. She was kicking me, banging deep into my ribs and stomach.

— How much longer, a man's voice said.

An engine raced. The lights were high beams. I crossed my hands over my face and curled up tight. We had come a long way together but she was moving on to something else now.

TEASE

Grampa knew one trick, but he had to be drunk to perform it. So he drank, starting early, hours before mother dropped us off. The minute she backed out of the driveway, he'd claw the air, grazing our faces. Then he'd poke his thumb through each blotchy fist.

"Got your nose! Yours too! Ha ha! Oh, what can you do?"

He'd move wildly about, twirling, waving his arms, creating a blur of our stolen noses. "See! Look! One of each. Go on," he'd say, "try and smell something."

We'd sniff the air and grab at our real noses. We'd wiggle and wrinkle them, not quite worried yet.

"Oh, you can still feel them," he'd say. "But that doesn't mean they're there."

So we'd race to the mirror to chase away our doubt.

"You think you see them," he'd say. "But that's only in your heads, a tired memory that refuses to fade, a cheap illusion like in the brains of limbless men who come back from war." Then he'd show us our poor noses, yellow and small, one in each hand.

"Hmm, I'm hungry. I think I'll eat these." And always my sister would cry.

She'd start slow, quietly sobbing, and then she'd wail: "No fun, no fair. I'm telling. Give us back our noses!"

He'd say, "No way! Now stop. No tears, or next I'll eat your eyes. Pop, pop! One, two!"

He'd chase her first, poor thing, every time, because she was tiny, wih bones like a bird. He'd lift her beneath one arm and tickle until she peed, then make her undress in front of the mirror, and I'd hear the whine of the bedroom door, and then her silence.

Sometimes an hour would creep past before he came out, his starched shirt soaked with sweat. "Now you," he'd say, in a breathless voice, raising his pinkies into devilish horns, grinning like death, knowing I wouldn't run. Because these are the eyes my grandmother gave me, and they could read him like a book.

DELETIONS

Later that night I drive back to her beach house, sneaking in like a thief to eliminate all clues, wiping for fingerprints, washing the dishes we used, pushing through a load of laundry, tidying here and there. Without witnesses, no one suspects the loot I gathered on my early visit, the skill of my entry, the urgency of my departure, or the extent of my cover up. I vacuum every room except the bedroom. She is breathing softly, curled like a question mark in the huge bed. She almost appears to be smiling. I tap her nose once, lightly, then tickle her chin until she gives off a tiny shudder in her sleep. I wait, and I watch her lips. At the first whisper of my name I breathe in the dreamy sound she makes. A criminal of the heart, I take back everything. Everything.

ENTOMOLOGY

Start tape:

On my arm this morning I discovered two fine looking specimens. One, slightly larger than the other, with the colorful markings of a male, climbed on top of the other, then beneath, then the two entangled to perform a brief buzzing rolling dance until the larger one rose up and flew away. For several minutes I watched the dazed female crawl around, jabbing her stinger, probing until she discovered a tender fleshy spot near my elbow. Within seconds she had burrowed down and in. By now I am almost numb to the sensation. The moment her head disappeared I used a red felt-tip pen to mark the area. I've learned that if I don't circle the wound immediately, the fever hazes over the event, and I wake up days later depending on the early signs of swelling to reveal the location of the new nest.

Stop tape.

SHIPWRECKED

The same day we buried the captain we salvaged the Victrola, though the cherry wood was ruined. Half of us put on dresses. And we danced.

THE CRICKET WAR

That summer an army of crickets started a war with my father. They picked a fight the minute they invaded our cellar. Dad didn't care for bugs much more than Mamma, but he could tolerate a few spiders and assorted creepy crawlers living in the basement. Every farmhouse had them. A part of rustic living, and something you needed to put up with if you wanted the simple life.

He told Mamma: Now that we're living out here, you can't be jerking your head and swallowing your gum over what's plain natural, Ellen. But Mamma was a city girl through and through and had no ears when it came to defending vermin. She said a cricket was no more than a noisy cockroach, just a dumb ugly bug that wouldn't shut up. She said in the city there were blocks of buildings overrun with cockroaches with no way for people to get rid of them. No sir, no way could she sleep with all that chirping going on; then to prove her point she wouldn't go to bed. She drank coffee and smoked my father's cigarettes and she paced between the couch and the TV. Next morning she threatened to pack up and leave, so Dad drove to the hardware store and hurried back. He squirted poison from a jug with a spray nozzle. He sprayed the basement and all around the foundation of the house. When he was finished he told us that was the end of it.

But what he should have said was: This is the beginning, the beginning of our war, the beginning of our destruction.

I often think back to that summer and try to imagine him delivering a speech with words like that, because for the next fourteen days mamma kept finding dead crickets in the

55

clean laundry. She'd shake out a towel or a sheet and a dead black cricket would roll across the linoleum. Sometimes the cat would corner one, and swat it around like he was playing hockey, then carry it away in his mouth. Dad said swallowing a few dead crickets wouldn't hurt as long as the cat didn't eat too many. Each time Mamma complained he told her it was only natural that we'd be finding a couple of dead ones for a while.

Soon live crickets started showing up in the kitchen and bathroom. Mamma freaked because she thought they were the dead crickets come back to haunt, but Dad said these was definitely a new batch, probably coming up on the pipes. He fetched his jug of poison and sprayed beneath the sink and behind the toilet and all along the baseboard until the whole house smelled of poison, and then he sprayed the cellar again, and then he went outside and sprayed all around the foundation leaving a foot-wide moat of poison. Stop them right in their tracks, he told us.

For a couple of weeks we went back to finding dead crickets in the laundry. Dad told us to keep a sharp look out. He suggested that we'd all be better off to hide as many as we could from Mamma. I fed a dozen to the cat who I didn't like because he scratched and bit for no reason. I hoped the poison might kill him so we could get a puppy.

Once in a while we found a dead cricket in the bathroom or beneath the kitchen sink. We didn't know if these were fresh dead or old dead the cat had played with and then abandoned. Dad cracked a few in half to show us that they were fresh. Then he used the rest of the poison to give the house another dose.

A couple of weeks later, when both live and dead crickets kept turning up, he emptied the cellar of junk. He borrowed Uncle Burt's pickup and hauled a load to the dump. Then he burned a lot of bundled newspapers and magazines which he said the crickets had turned into nests.

He stood over that fire with a rake in one hand and a garden hose in the other. He wouldn't leave it even when Mamma sent me out to fetch him for supper. He wouldn't leave the fire, and Mamma wouldn't put our supper on the table. Both my brothers were crying. Finally she went out and got him herself. And while we ate, the wind lifted some embers onto the woodpile. The only gasoline was in the lawn mower's fuel tank but that was enough to create an explosion big enough to reach the house. Once the roof caught, there wasn't much anyone could do.

After the fire trucks left I made the mistake of volunteering to stay behind while Mamma took the others to Aunt Gail's. I helped Dad and Uncle Burt and two men I'd never seen before carry things out of the house and stack them by the road. In the morning we'd come back in Burt's truck and haul everything away. We worked late into the night and we didn't talk much, hardly a word about anything that mattered, and Dad didn't offer any plan that he might have for us now.

Uncle Burt passed a bottle around, but I shook my head when it came to me. I kicked and picked through the mess, dumbstruck at how little there was to salvage, while all around the roar of crickets magnified our silence.

ROOMS FOR RENT, MEN ONLY

My first night in that cramped, attic room I didn't sleep. Not a wink. I simply lay on my back, still as a corpse, sunk deep into the bowed, rank smelling mattress. I kept the light on, a lousy 25 watt bulb, and I studied the water stains on the slanted ceiling. I thought about a great number of things, including my wife, while listening to the sounds of mice scurrying through the walls. Of course, I didn't know they were mice. The landlady hadn't mentioned any rodent problem, so like a fool I mistook the scratchy noise for the tapping of summer rain upon the roof.

The room was a windowless space adjacent to a filthy kitchen shared by eight other roomers, all men, all of us running away from something. Each night mice traveled past my room and squeezed though holes and cracks to raid our kitchen. Previous roomers had plugged many of these entrances with cardboard and scraps of wood, but they hadn't gotten all of them, and each night the mice came and went pretty much as they pleased.

Every morning we would assess the damage — the half-gnawed boxes of corn flakes, oatmeal, pasta. We'd follow the path of mouse droppings back to some new entry point. Then seal that hole as best we could.

There was more to it, of course. The agonizing day-to-day, the petty arguments and drunken fights. Sometimes a death due to a heart attack, or an overdose. But essentially that is how we lived, tracing trails of mouse shit, discovering holes then blocking them, setting traps, spreading poison, working collectively, until someone moved out or got themselves evicted, or returned to his wife, leaving the rest of us to carry on, battling things we could not see.

THE BARTENDER STORY

You're at an office party, telling a joke. The joke begins like a thousand others. A man walks into a bar. Or two men. A rabbi and a priest. Or two women. A prostitute and a nun. Maybe an elephant and a chimpanzee.

What's important is the bartender greets each patron with a warm smile. He's overly friendly because business has been bad. Nothing like the days when he first bought the place. Back then, on theater nights, flocks poured in. The crowds were avant-garde, chic; everyone had manners and style.

Now the only customers he gets are props, puppet performers, mere stooges, the loath deliverers of tired jokes. Sometimes this makes the bartender feel like an accomplice. At other times, a fool. Between jokes he tries to remember his dreams. Did he always want to be a bartender?

On your worst days, you think about taking a mixology course and becoming a bartender. You've heard the pay is bad but the tips are good.

On his worst days the bartender believes he might prefer to be on the other side, coming and going, reciting punch lines.

You tell the part of the joke where he asks, "What will it be? What can I get you? What'll you have?"

The anatomy of the joke requires him to utter one of these phrases. He has some liberty, but how much he doesn't know. No one tells the bartender anything. He is never in on the joke.

Using a dirty rag to wipe the bar, he awaits a response that will propel this latest rendering of the joke forward, understanding he may never make another sale. Likewise, you understand this tired joke may not get a laugh. Not with this group.

You decide that after you deliver the punch line, you'll go home, jerk off, go to bed.

Likewise, after you deliver the punch line, the bartender will duck into the windowless smoke-filled backroom where there is a lady with orange peels in her hair, a dozen patron saints playing pool, and a bug-eyed office worker with amnesia who used to be a writer. No joke.

eBay BOOK AUCTION

One man's life.
Hard cover.
No jacket.
No yellowing of pages.
No markings.
Some fraying of edges.
Minor damage to spine.
Half-moon coffee cup ring stain on back.
Otherwise clean.

DEADBOLT

First time she walked in and caught me, I had the December issue spread across my lap.

'Oh my god,' she said.

Not my fault, really. It was a cheap three-room apartment with no lock on the bathroom door.

The next afternoon she came home with a dead bolt. I was on the couch, stretched out, watching TV. For the first time ever, Larry and Curly were ganging up on Moe.

'Feet off the furniture, mister.'

I wiggled my toes. 'No shoes,' I said.

She put her purse beside the Chinese lamp on top of the TV.

'Those socks are what I'm talking about. I can smell them from here,' she said.

Soon as I sat up, she underhand tossed the deadbolt. It hit the back of the couch, then landed right where my head had been.

'Turn this shit off and put that doohickey on the bathroom door,' she said.

The instructions were printed in the smallest type I'd ever seen. I studied the pictures labeled one, two, three. We didn't own a screwdriver, so I used a butter knife. The wood was warped and I had trouble lining the thing up.

I shut the door and worked the bolt back and forth a few times. It was a tight fit but good enough.

I opened the door and said 'Come and see.' I could hear voices, people shouting on TV. 'Hey,' I said.

'Not now. I'm watching my shows.'

This was in the days when soap operas played one after the other all through the afternoon.

So I locked myself inside. I pulled the December issue from beneath the tub, dropped my pants to my ankles and sat on the toilet.

A little while later she rattled the doorknob. Then she banged the door and made it shake.

'Put your shoulder into it,' I said.

AUTHOR SIGNING

Not counting store personnel, nine people attended the reading. After which, only one member of the audience purchased my novel. He was a dull looking fellow in suspender overalls and dirty work boots; an outfit that a plumber or a painter might wear. He approached with the book open in one hand so that the covers flopped like wings. He rifled the pages. I felt a whiff of air.

God, I wish I could do what you do, he said. I'd love to write for a living.

I smiled and removed the cap from my pen.

If only he had to do what I had to do, I thought. Every day. That and only that. Would he call it living? Swapping my life for his, he'd want to trade right back, reverse the switch, keep his sorrowful existence.

He presented the book and held it steady as I scribbled my signature. He thanked me. The flutter in his voice sounded quite sincere. I shook his hand.

As he walked away, I considered the back of him. He had my book tucked under one arm. No bag. No receipt in his hand. Had he even paid for the book? Thief or not, I admired his unconstrained, uninhibited, unhurried gait. Given the opportunity, I'd cling to his common dullness better than he ever could.

HER K BIBLE

Shortly before she ran off to join the Army, my sister Darla went cuckoo from reading Kafka, Carver, Salinger, and Joyce.

She considered Carver's work "clearly" everything Joyce's wasn't. And vice versa.

And Salinger's "attempts", she decided, were just silly notes to the teacher, "ill-mannered, deliberately discordant, and uncomfortably sexually aloof." At that time I liked Salinger and was prepared to fight. But she surrendered too easily, and later confessed she actually felt sorry for the man. All things considered, she believed it the best thing for everyone that Jerome had stopped publishing the exact moment he had.

But Kafka, whom I had not read, drove her straight over the edge. At seventeen, she fell into Kafkaesque dreams and fantasies. She razored her red hair short as a boy's, took to living in a long grey overcoat, rain or shine, and carrying a huge book of blank pages, a sort of diary to-be, that she called her K Bible.

She powdered her face to hide her freckles, drank twenty to thirty glasses of water a day, ate nothing while in the presence of others; and one night, at dinner, when my mother asked how long she planned to continue on this insane diet, Darla said: While you sleep, mother, I eat the mice in the walls, I eat the moth larvae in your sweater box, I pick at the dust mites crawling on your pillow, and I collect the dark purple scabs that fall from the dried scratches your claws have ripped into my brother's tender back.

My mother said: You! You stop! You leave him out of it!

I flinched and said, What did I do, when did I become a part of this story?

She handed me her book, my thin sister did. She showed me her K bible — all the pages adorned with my flesh.

FOR WEASEL EYES ONLY

My grandpa was searching for a missing hen when he found the notes of a weasel behind his barn. Scratchy, scrubby, paw-printed memoranda. Barely readable if you ask me: just a scattering of feathers and blood and claw marks in the soil But grandpa was a genius of sorts, a man who could read a thing that made no complete sense.

"You see these marks," grandpa said. "These markings are meant for another weasel."

Turns out a weasel knew things an owl didn't. Because there were notes on how to capture a hawk when the moon is cracked in two. Notes on bears and bees and bush berry treats. Notes on insects that glowed, and the fish they attached themselves to, and how quiet air dances with rain, and bruising sky creates thunder. There were even notes on weasel death: crude sketches with dashed and dotted lines showing an owl's sweeping assault with a cartoon lightening bolt in its wake.

Grandpa left everything untouched, saying: "The little buggers get smarter every year and harder for me to catch."

Old grandpa is dead now, like a lot of old smart men. That weasel too, I'm afraid, is long deceased. Though, the crafty owl remains a stuffed, dusty toy in my dank and muggy attic. Shot clean by grandma the winter it coughed up the bones of a newborn kitten in the snow.

But the weasel notes are mine. All of them.

TESTAMENT

His eyes were closed but he wasn't sleeping. The lids had begun to crust over from lack of use. He had shut them days ago, after vowing to his wife never to open them again.

He knew where he was but not how he had gotten there.

'Pulse normal,' a voice said.

Something wrapped high on his arm began to seize and tighten.

Someone removed his shoe from his left foot. They peeled his sock off as well. He expected the right shoe to go next. Instead he felt something rake upward along his bare sole. His leg jerked involuntarily.

'One-twenty over eighty,' someone said.

The band on his arm hissed as it relaxed its grip.

'Okay. Wheel him down to x-ray and get me some pictures.'

Then he was moving, glad to be moving. Within seconds the air tasted better.

He stopped for a while and la-la music tickled his ears. The air grew stale. He wondered where his wife was, if she were close by wringing her hands in anguish.

Then he was moving again. He breathed slow and steadily through his nose and tried to keep his nostrils from flaring. He was moving now at a pretty good clip but he wished he could go faster. There were bumps in the road all the way.

SWEET DEAL

My father wasn't home fifteen minutes when I heard the screen door slam. He came off the porch with a sour look on his face. My mother was inside, screaming. I held the ball and watched him walk directly beneath the basket. He shook his head at me. Behind the garage was the small shed where he kept his gear. He trained horses when he could get the work. He stopped suddenly, twisted around and clapped his hands. "One shot," he said.

I was less than half his height. I lobbed the ball high and he caught it awkwardly by his hip. He held it in front of his chest with both hands and looked at the seams. "Your mother is nuts," he said, "But I guess you already know that." He threw the ball, a crisp bounce pass that skipped off the blacktop and came up quick, right to my chest.

"Like that," he said. " Elbow and wrist. Make it snap."

I adjusted my hands and pushed. The ball bounced once, a pathetic bounce, and he caught it near his ankles. He was crouched on the three-point line I'd measured with chalk on a string. In one smooth motion he sprang, rose up, extended his arms, and executed a jump shot. The ball arced higher than the roof of the garage, then dropped straight through the hoop, touching nothing but net.

"Wow," I said, and raced to retrieve the ball.

"Too close," he said, and retreated so quickly I thought he might be leaving.

He clapped his hands and I skip-passed the ball to him.

"From here?" he said.

"Bet you can't," I yelled.

But then he did.

All afternoon my father sank high arching shots from well beyond the line.

THE THIRTEENTH DREAM

For Jessica

Your father, the writer, whom you promised your mother you would not read, whose books, though obscure, you find dark, purposefully vague, as though he is determined from the onset to confuse even the most faithful reader with ill placed references to prior works, i.e. old rhyming poems you once memorized but have now forgotten, alluding, as your father sometimes will, to comments critics have offered in courtroom testimony, private letters, short memos, and far too many hastily scribbled caustic phrases penned on crumpled napkins, notes meant for him and him alone, filed as serious sagely almost Kafkaesque advice, professionally polite, never meant to offend, all of which he later publishes anyway under a less than assumed pseudonym and then denies having any knowledge of, later threatening to sue, crying foul, foul, screaming in your dreams that you, his one and only daughter, are witness to the atrocities, the plot conducted against him, the very theft of you, his first born child, you and you alone, the soul witness whose duty, whose obligation it is for the sake of aesthetic freedom to right these wrongs not on his behalf, no, hardly for him, nor the work he calls his craft, but because justice demands, simple old fashioned justice necessitates your father the writer call you up, long distance, bed to bed, dream to dream, disturbing the quiet pre-dawn promise of an almost perfect morning, waking you from slumber you have worked for and earned, then he startles, alarming you with a voice so familiar you believe for a moment that it is not him but you, your own voice echoing in the dream you have had a dozen times since childhood and are having again, now, for the thirteenth time, this, the meaningless thirteenth dream, the memory of which you take to your therapist, spilling your guts, weeping, plucking tissues three, four at a time, the absolute hardest memory to deal with because you're convinced such feeling wouldn't lie, certain it will be the last time your father uses this scheme to try and reach you, to touch you, to comfort with anything more than words on a page written for a child, a lost child, his own, the heartbreak he won't forget.

QUARTER OF MIDNIGHT

My mother was dying again, though this time for real. Hospice had her heavily medicated and resting comfortably in an old brick and mortar building that used to be a convent. They gave an estimate of hours or days.

Waiting for the news was beginning to take its toll. Every twenty minutes I checked the battery level on my cell phone. Reading, writing, even thinking was out of the question, because it's true what they say: you only get one mother in this life.

I couldn't sleep so I walked three blocks to a diner for a midnight breakfast.

There was one other customer, a fat man eating an English muffin.

The menu was a blackboard above the grill, everything written in cursive with pink chalk. Only the prices were clear.

While I was deciding what to order, the fat man said, Do you know how to make coffee?

The waitress, who was a peroxide blonde with a mouthful of chewing gum, leaned left, looking past me.

She said, I gave you coffee. You're drinking it.

This, darling, is not coffee, the fat man said.

The waitress blew a bubble, let it snap. She gave me a look like I knew her shoes were too tight and her varicose veins made her legs ache.

What's yours, she said.

I pretended to study the menu board but all I could think of was how I am not bothered writing stories about unremarkable people living unremarkable lives while I kill time waiting for my mother to die.

DONATION

Yesterday I stuffed some words in a sack and gave them to the poor. That is to say I filled a garbage bag with a couple of shredded manuscripts then stuffed the bag into a donation bin outside a local mall.

Painted on the front of the huge yellow bin, which resembled a dumpster, was: SHOES AND CLOTHING FOR THE NEEDY.

To hell with that, I thought. Let the poor dress themselves in nouns and verbs. Let them weave garments for their children based on the things I've said.

Acknowledgements

Masquerade / DIAGRAM, Oct. 2002 / & DIAGRAM Anthology. Del Sol Press, 2003.
Author Signing / Rumble, August 2006
No Harm Done / Rumble, Feb. 2006, & Rumble Micro Fiction Anthology
Something To Remember You By / Rumble, May 2007
Balloon Man / "Ten Fictions" Turnrow, March 2003
The Last Trash Can / "Ten Fictions" Turnrow, March 2003
My New Place / "Ten Fictions" Turnrow, March 2003
Never In A Million Years / "Ten Fictions" Turnrow, March 2003
Repeat As Necessary / "Ten Fictions" Turnrow, March 2003
Grave Invitation / "Ten Fictions" Turnrow, March 2003
Float / "Ten Fictions" Turnrow, March 2003
Duck Walk / "9 Fictions" Oasis Magazine, July 2002
Blind Date / "9 Fictions" Oasis Magazine, July 2002
Grays / "9 Fictions" Oasis Magazine, July 2002
Minimalism At The Beach / Linnaean Street (Spring 2000 Prix de Linnaeus.)
Deletions / In Posse Review
History Lesson / The-Phone-Book, (UK story project for mobile devices)
Signal Fire / The-Phone-Book,
Entomology / The-Phone-Book
eBay Book Auction / The-Phone-Book
Day 59 / The-Phone-Book
Shipwrecked / Hint Fiction Anthology
Her Ex-Boyfriend's eMail / The-Phone-Book
Last Time I Saw My Father / The-Phone-Book
Absolution / "Best 50 stories" The Phone Book
Wishes / Elimae 2007
Three Days Of Mourning / The-Phone-Book
Heart / The-Phone-Book
Membrane / The-Phone-Book
New Mother / The-Phone-Book
Redemption Sale / The-Phone-Book
The Seventies / The-Phone-Book,
Crybabies / The-Phone-Book,
Dirty Laundry / The-Phone-Book,
Biology Lesson / The-Phone-Book,
A Yard Full Of Birds / Vestal Review (Spring 2002 / Reader's Choice Award , April 2002
Shuteye / Cafe Irreal, (Issue 15, August 2005)
Donation / In Posse Review
Her K Bible / "Three Fictions" The God Particle, Nov. 2002
Tarzan's Dream / Diagram 2008
Six Crows / In Which (Vol. 1, Number 3—Fall 2001)
The Lion Tamer's Wife / elimae, August 2008
For Weasel Eyes Only / Eclectica, Nov. 2001
The Thirteenth Dream / 3 a.m. Magazine, Nov. 2002
Tease / Saga City, Nov. 2002
The Bartender Story / Café Irreal, November 2009
Sweet Deal / Flash Fiction Magazine, April 2010
Deadbolt / Flash Fiction Magazine, April 2010
Testament / Flash Fiction Magazine, April 2010
Quarter of Midnight / Six Little Things, April 2010
Deathbed Notes / nth Word, December 2010
Lord Have Mercy / nth Word, April 2010
Rooms for Rent, Men Only / Liquid Imagination, January 2011

ABOUT THE AUTHOR:

Bob Thurber grew up in Rhode Island. He admits to having been "a deeply distracted, hyper-anxious, terribly bad student" who graduated high school by "the skin of his teeth." He has no degrees in anything and never attended a writing class. He worked independently at writing every day for 20 years before attempting to publish.

Over the last decade Bob Thurber's short fiction has received a long list of literary awards, prizes and citations, including The Barry Hannah Fiction Prize. He is the author of "Paperboy: A Dysfunctional Novel." His work has appeared in two dozen anthologies and he's been called a "master of micro fiction," an "emotional terrorist," and "The Sam Peckinpah of Flash Fiction." He resides in Massachusetts, and though you should most certainly avoid him at all costs, you might do well to track his whereabouts and learn more of his transgressions at: **www.BobThurber.net**

Made in the USA
Columbia, SC
25 August 2018